Beverly Beaver's Hats

⸺⸱⸱❧❧⸱⸱⸺

An Adirondack Tale

Story by Joan Cofrancesco

Illustrations by Janine Bartolotti

AuthorHouse™
1663 Liberty Drive
Bloomington, IN 47403
www.authorhouse.com
Phone: 1 (800) 839-8640

Published by AuthorHouse 04/14/2016

ISBN: 978-1-5246-0421-9 (sc)
ISBN: 978-1-5246-0422-6 (e)

authorHOUSE®

This book is dedicated to my mother

who made hats for her friends and family.

Beverly Beaver loved to knit.

She made curtains that hung and seat covers that fit.

She made afghans and sweaters and little red mitts.

She loved to create. She just hated to sit.

One day Michael Mole came to her Adirondack house.

It was near Lake Placid and next to Ms. Mouse.

"My head gets cold when I dig through the ground."

She looked at his head and turned him around.

"Come back in a day and I'll show you a hat."

He thanked her and left and went on his way.

She knitted and knitted and when he came back

She gave him the best brown hat that looked like a sack.

"This will keep me warm. Thank you so much."

Everyone in Eagle Bay saw it and wanted one too,

Sally Squirrel,

Sandy Snake,

Sandy Snake,

and Kelly Kangaroo.

They lined up for miles outside her little shack.

There was Lily Lizard

and Kevin Cat.

She knitted and knitted 'til one day she saw

Peter Porcupine come from Whiteface Mount.

"I need a hat, Ms. Beaver, to wear to the Lake Dance.

I want it blue and I want it fast."

"I have a date for Saturday and I want to look good.

It's very important, if you only could?"

Ms. Beaver was baffled.

She didn't know what to do.

His head's full of needles.

She worked until two.

With hats piled before her—not one would do.

She cried and cried, "What shall I do?"

Finally she fell asleep and dreamt of a hat.

It was blue and big and had holes in a batch.

When she woke up, she made it in no time flat.

When Peter returned, Beverly showed him the hat.

He smiled and said, "Why will you just look at that.

It's the best hat I've ever seen."

He put it on and he looked like a dream.

Beverly thought my, what a handsome brute.

And he said, "I have one more request for you."

"What is it?" she asked, "What could it be?"

"I hope it won't keep me up 'til quarter to three."

"No, Ms. Beaver, that's not it at all. I'll ask you once

but I won't ask you twice

would you be my date for the Lake Dance tonight?"

"Of course I will…but what will I wear? I haven't a hat."

He looked at the pile of hats on the ground

and handed her a red, floppy hat.

She put it on and that was that.

The End

CPSIA information can be obtained
at www.ICGtesting.com
Printed in the USA
LVHW071656180222
711485LV00028B/2048